SURVIVAL

Hurricane!

Frieda Wishinsky

Illustrated by
Don Kilby

Scholastic Canada Ltd.

Toronto New York London Auckland Sydney
Mexico City New Delhi Hong Kong Buenos Aires

Scholastic Canada Ltd.
604 King Street West, Toronto, Ontario M5V 1E1, Canada

Scholastic Inc.
557 Broadway, New York, NY 10012, USA

Scholastic Australia Pty Limited
PO Box 579, Gosford, NSW 2250, Australia

Scholastic New Zealand Limited
Private Bag 94407, Botany, Manukau 2163, New Zealand

Scholastic Children's Books
Euston House, 24 Eversholt Street, London NW1 1DB, UK

www.scholastic.ca

Library and Archives Canada Cataloguing in Publication
Wishinsky, Frieda, author
      Hurricane! : the fury of Hurricane Hazel / Frieda Wishinsky ;
illustrations by Don Kilby.
(Survival)
Issued in print and electronic formats.
ISBN 978-1-4431-4644-9 (paperback).--ISBN 978-1-4431-4645-6 (html)
      I. Kilby, Don, illustrator II. Title. III. Series: Wishinsky, Frieda.
Survival.
PS8595.I834H8 2015   jC813'.54   C2015-906484-8
                        C2015-906485-6

Photo credits: Cover: house ©Victor Zastolskiy/Shutterstock, Inc.; waves:
©Ronnie Chua/Shutterstock, Inc.; storm background: ©isoga/Shutterstock,
Inc.; car: ©Aleksandar Todorovic/Shutterstock, Inc.; background map:
©Bulletin of the American Meteorological Society, Vol. 36, No. 6 (1955).
Page 99: ©Weston Historical Society, Weston, Ontario.

6 5 4 3 2 1   Printed in Canada 121   16 17 18 19 20

MIX
Paper from
responsible sources
FSC
www.fsc.org FSC® C004071

For my friend Rebecca Upjohn, with thanks

CHAPTER ONE

October 16, 1954

Michael climbed onto the rickety chair. As he leaned toward the attic window, the chair snapped. Michael tumbled into a box. His right shoulder smashed into a sharp edge.

The floor creaked and heaved. The rain drummed on the roof. The wind howled around him.

His hands trembled as he pulled over the other wobbly chair. He held on to it with one hand and yanked himself up with the other.

"Michael, where are you? What happened?" His mother's frantic voice rose above the pelting rain.

"Michael! Hurry!" called Paul. "I think the water's rising higher in the house."

Michael's heart was beating so hard he couldn't think. He peered out the window. Paul leaned against the wet shingles and clung to the pipe. His mother crouched on the roof above Paul and held on tightly to the TV antenna. Their faces dripped with the pounding rain. The wind snapped against their clothing.

Someone screamed from below.

"Help me! Please!"

More screams pierced the darkness. Screams echoed over the rain and wind.

"Go, Michael!" called his mother. "Now!"

Michael could barely breathe.

He lowered himself out the window feet first. His rear end dragged along the slippery shingles. As he made his way slowly toward his mother and Paul, Michael's right foot slid on a loose shingle.

He was sliding!

He reached for something — anything — to stop

him from falling off the roof, but there was nothing to hold on to. Nothing.

He fell into the darkness and splashed into the icy water.

CHAPTER TWO

October 15, 1954

Michael pulled on his rubber boots. "Come on, Paul," he said to his best friend. "We have to hurry! We're going to be late for school."

Paul dumped his overnight bag in Michael's front closet. His mom had just dropped him off. The boys took turns sleeping over at each other's house every Friday night, and he was staying at Michael's that night.

They waved goodbye to Michael's mom and ran out the door.

It had been raining so hard for the last three days that the front lawn was as squishy as a wet sponge. Puddles covered the sidewalks and streets of the neighbourhood. The boys turned to cross the street just as a car zoomed by, shooting water into the air like a geyser. They jumped back, but it was too late. They were drenched up to their knees.

Paul shivered. He pulled the hood of his raincoat over his head. "I've never seen so much rain."

Michael brushed his wet hair out of his eyes. "Maybe we're getting hit by Hurricane Hazel. I've been reading about hurricanes for the speech contest next week."

Paul laughed. "I bet you've read every book in the library on hurricanes already. Remember when you spoke about volcanoes for the grade five contest last year? You knew everything about volcanoes."

"Reading is easy. Speaking is hard. I wish I didn't have to get up in front of the class. It gives me a stomach ache."

"Yeah, but your speech was interesting. And everyone loved it when your volcano exploded."

Michael rolled his eyes. "It wasn't supposed to explode *that* much. That was embarrassing."

"Well, you're not exploding anything this year, right? Don't worry. Your speech will be good. You're great at researching."

Michael sighed. He hoped Paul was right. He loved learning about natural disasters like volcanoes, tornadoes, earthquakes or hurricanes. Everything happened so quickly and changed in a flash. He even liked writing stories and reports. But speaking in front of the class was different.

Last year, as soon as Miss Murray called on him to present his speech, his stomach began to ache. When he stood up to walk to the front of the class, his legs began to shake. They wouldn't stop shaking the whole time he spoke. But that wasn't all. As he spoke, his voice was low, and he kept coughing and clearing his throat all through his speech. He was sure everyone noticed.

And then things got worse. Michael showed the class his papier mâché model volcano, but instead of lava just dripping down the sides, it blew up all over Miss Murray's desk. It splattered the blackboard, the floor and even Miss Murray's dress. Michael's face turned as red as his lava.

Miss Murray had been nice about it and so had the janitor who came to clean up the mess. But Jim and Ian had teased him for a week after the contest.

And now, in just one week, Michael had to stand up in front of his sixth-grade class and present again. Every time he thought about it, he felt like someone had punched him in the stomach.

Another car whizzed by, splashing water onto the sidewalk. This time the boys jumped out of the way before getting soaked.

"What's your topic this year?" Michael asked, as they skirted puddles and hurried down the wet streets.

"Sharks," said Paul.

Michael laughed. "I should have guessed *that*. Last year you talked about giant squid and octopuses. You really love the sea."

"Yeah, my mom says that's because I was born in Vancouver and you could see the ocean from our apartment. I don't remember that, of course. I was only two when we moved to Toronto. All I know is that I love everything about the sea. And sharks are amazing. I saw two giant ones on a boat tour when we visited my aunt in British Columbia last year. I can't wait to tell everybody about *that*."

Paul grinned. He liked public speaking. Last year he had come in third in the speech contest.

Michael wished he felt comfortable speaking, too.

Paul looked at his watch. "Yikes! It's getting late. Let's take the footbridge across the river. We'll get to school faster that way."

"The footbridge? It will be slippery with all this rain. My dad keeps warning me not to cross it. He says it's not safe."

"That's what my parents say, too. But everyone at school crosses the bridge, and nothing bad has ever happened to anyone. We'll be fine."

"I know, but . . ."

"If we don't cross the footbridge, we won't make it to school on time."

Michael sighed. "Okay." He took a deep breath.

It's just a small bridge, he told himself. *It only takes a few minutes to cross it.*

"Hurry!" Paul called again, racing toward the bridge.

The rain pelted down. Leaves, branches and debris littered the ground.

Michael shivered as a cold blast of wind almost knocked off his hood. He tightened his hood to keep the water from running down his back.

They weren't far now. He could see the bridge! It was higher than he remembered. And the Humber River churned below it.

Two boys stood on the bridge. They shouted to each other as they bounced up and down on the surface.

It was hard to see their faces through the pounding, blinding rain. They jumped up and down again and again, each time going higher. They laughed and shoved each other toward the edge of the bridge. They bent over the sides and looked down at the fast-moving river. Then they ran to the other side of the bridge.

They stood near the end of the bridge yelling to Michael and Paul, but it was hard to hear what they were saying.

Paul reached the bridge first. "Michael. Look! It's Jim and Ian. They're waiting for us."

Michael's stomach twisted. Now he recognized them! Jim lived a few blocks away from Michael.

Michael wished they could turn around and take the long way to school. But they couldn't turn back now. If they didn't cross the bridge they'd be late for school. Worse than that, Jim and Ian would tell everyone they were scared.

CHAPTER THREE

Paul hurried ahead onto the bridge. But as soon as he stepped on it, he slid on a pile of wet leaves. He landed on his rear end, and Jim and Ian pointed and laughed. But Paul didn't look at them. He scrambled up and kept walking.

Jim and Ian stared at Michael now instead.

Paul was halfway across the bridge when Michael began to cross. Each step made Michael's heart race faster and his chest tighten. He stopped walking for a minute and took a deep breath. Then he started walking again.

He took more steps. And more. The Humber roared below. The river sounded so close, so fast. Every time it crashed against the sides of the bridge, it felt like the bridge was moving, shifting. Michael glanced down. The water was rising. It looked like it might rise above the surface of the bridge!

He took another step and another. The bridge felt endless.

Don't think. Keep walking.

The surface of the bridge was slippery. It was carpeted in clumps of leaves and broken branches. Michael kept his eyes down. He walked slowly, carefully, trying not to slide. He didn't want to fall.

How far am I from the end now?

He looked up. He was only halfway across. Paul stood at the end of the bridge. He pointed to his watch. He signalled to Michael to hurry up.

Jim and Ian stood under a large maple tree. Their eyes were focused on Michael. Michael could see them clearly now — especially Jim, who towered over his shorter friend.

"Hey, Michael. What's taking you so long?" shouted Jim, cupping his hands around his mouth to make himself heard over the howling wind and rain. "Are you scared?"

"I'm not scared," said Michael, but he knew he sounded scared.

"Can't hear you, Michael," Jim called back.

"He said he's not scared," shouted Paul. "And he's not."

"Yeah, right!" said Jim, poking Ian in the ribs and guffawing.

Don't look at them. Don't listen to them. Keep walking.

Wet leaves, sharp, pointy twigs, broken pinecones

swirled into Michael's face, blinding him. He hunched his shoulders and shielded his eyes as more debris flew at him. Below, the river rumbled. It felt like it would slosh over the bridge at any moment.

"He's scared as a baby," shouted Ian.

"Baby, baby, kindergarten baby," chanted Jim.

"Stop it. Leave Michael alone." Paul's voice rose above the other two boys.

"You're going to be late," said Jim, laughing. "Michael will never make it across in time."

Michael's face burned. He hated how Jim and Ian made him feel.

The rain slammed into his face, blurring his vision. But he kept moving. He walked faster and faster.

Finally he was off the bridge! He leaned against its concrete supports. He rubbed his eyes. "Everything was flying around. I couldn't see where I was going."

"I know," said Paul. "Maybe we shouldn't have crossed the bridge today. But we made it. Come on!

We don't have much time before the bell rings."

Michael peered around. "Where are Jim and Ian?"

"They didn't want to be late, so they took off. I told them you'd make it across in time and you did. We'd better run now to make it before the bell."

"Okay," said Michael. "Let's go!"

CHAPTER FOUR

The boys raced the last few blocks to school. They rushed into their class as the bell rang.

Jim and Ian were already in their seats. When Michael and Paul arrived, Jim and Ian made faces and shot spitballs at them.

The spitballs missed.

"We'll get you next time," said Jim, as Michael and Paul hung their wet coats on the hooks beside all the others. Black, blue and rainbow-coloured umbrellas leaned against the back wall.

The friends slid into their seats beside each other as their teacher, Mr. Briggs, dashed in. His jacket and hair were soaked. He pulled a clean handkerchief out of his desk drawer and tried drying his hair, but his hair was too wet and his handkerchief too small to dry anything.

"Here's my morning saying for today, class: *Listen to good suggestions.*" Mr. Briggs grinned. "My wife told me to take an umbrella today, but my hands were full and I was sure the rain would finally let up! I guess it didn't."

The kids laughed.

Every morning Mr. Briggs mentioned a favourite expression. Sometimes he made up his own. He'd announce it to the class after telling them a story or explaining an assignment. Yesterday he said, "Read all about it," after encouraging them to use a variety of resources to research their topics for their speeches.

Michael had already read five books and a bunch of newspaper articles about hurricanes. He'd written down his ideas, and last night he'd started practising his speech in front of the mirror on his dresser. He hoped practising would help him feel less nervous about speaking in front of the class.

He'd also been following the latest hurricane — Hazel — as it ripped through the Caribbean. Hazel was barrelling north after hammering the Carolinas in the US. It would be perfect to end his talk about hurricanes with Hazel.

"Let's go around the room, and you can each tell me what you'll be speaking about next week," said Mr. Briggs. "Let's start with you, Jim."

"Motorcycles," said Jim, flashing a thumbs-up sign to Ian. "Best topic ever!"

Ian flashed him a V-for-victory sign.

"Good topic, Jim," said Mr. Briggs. "Mary?"

"Stars."

"Movie stars?" asked Mr. Briggs.

Mary shook her head. "No. Real stars. Up in the sky."

Mr. Briggs smiled. "Excellent. Michael?"

"Hurricanes."

"Perfect timing with all this rain. We're lucky in Toronto that we don't get hurricanes."

"If we did, Michael would be hiding under his bed," snickered Jim.

"There's no need for remarks like that, Jim," snapped Mr. Briggs.

Michael's face turned red.

"Sorry, sir," murmured Jim, but he didn't sound sorry at all.

"Don't let him get to you," Paul whispered to Michael. "You know Jim. He wants to win the contest."

Michael nodded. Jim had been bragging about winning for the last two weeks.

"Michael, I know how much you enjoy researching and how good you are it," said Mr. Briggs. "Can you tell the class your favourite way to learn about a new topic?"

"Yeah. Tell us, smarty pants," whispered Jim, from two rows behind him.

Mr. Briggs shot Jim a look. Jim slunk down in his seat.

Michael talked about how he took out a bunch of books from the library and read newspaper articles. Some kids then discussed how they interviewed people for their research. After that Mr. Briggs gave them forty-five minutes to work on their speeches.

It was still raining hard when the recess bell rang.

"Indoor recess!" said Mr. Briggs. "I have to speak to Miss James for a few minutes. But I'll be right here, just outside the classroom door. Keep the noise down."

Mr. Briggs walked to the door to speak to the vice-principal. As soon as his back was turned, Jim stood up and called, "Hey, everybody, watch this!" A few kids turned around. Jim kept his voice low so Mr. Briggs wouldn't hear. Then he put his hands on the back of two chairs and made his legs go wobbly. "That's Michael walking across the footbridge over the Humber. What a chicken!"

Ian guffawed.

"You're not so brave yourself," said Paul. "I saw you jump out of your seat when we had that thunderstorm a few weeks ago."

"That's a lie," snarled Jim, as Mr. Briggs turned back to the class.

"Thanks, Paul," whispered Michael, as they began a game of checkers.

"Hey, we stick up for each other. You stood up for me when Jim pushed me out of the way so he and Ian could get the best spot for catch at recess."

"They still got the best spot."

"I know, but at least you told them to quit shoving us around. But who cares about them? We're playing Monopoly tonight. I plan to buy lots of property. I'm going to win *big*."

Michael smiled. Every Friday since school began they'd played Monopoly at their sleepovers. They kept track of how many games they'd each won. Right now the score was tied. Michael was determined to break the tie tonight. He couldn't wait.

CHAPTER FIVE

As soon as the last bell rang, Michael and Paul darted out of class.

The rain fell even harder than it had in the morning. The wind whipped against their raincoats and blew blinding rain into their faces.

"This crazy rain's not stopping. It's just getting worse. There's no way I want to take the bridge now," said Michael.

"Yeah. My rear end is still sore from my fall," said Paul.

The boys crossed the street and slogged on. Around them, people hurried home clutching bags and bundles close to keep them dry. The puddles on the sidewalks and streets were growing larger, wider and deeper by the minute. Cars and buses plowed through the water, shooting waves onto the sidewalks, drenching everything and everyone.

Michael tried wiping the rain off his nose with his wet hands, but it was useless. He couldn't wait to get home and take off his wet clothes. Everything clung to him like glue. Every part of him was damp and cold. Beside him Paul huddled into his raincoat.

The wind blew so hard now it was difficult to stand up straight. It was hard not to get pushed into a pole or a parked car. The sky turned darker and the steely grey clouds hovered above, thick and heavy.

Halfway home the wind picked up with even more force, bending branches, knocking down garbage cans and rattling mailboxes. Broken twigs, wet newspapers and clumps of autumn leaves swirled around Michael and Paul.

A muddy, wet page of a newspaper flew into Michael's face. "Yuck," he groaned, pulling it off.

A metal garbage can slammed into Paul's leg.

"Ouch!" he cried. He bent over and rubbed his leg. "That hurts!"

"Can you walk?" asked Michael.

"Yeah, sort of. What a day! First my rear end and now my leg. This rain is vicious!" Paul took a step and winced.

"Oh no!" called a woman up ahead, as her umbrella slipped out of her hands. Michael raced after it, but it flew up like a balloon and sailed over the trees before he could grab it.

"Thanks," the woman said. "That's the second umbrella I've lost this week. When will the rain stop?" She hunched her shoulders and rushed off.

The boys bent over trying to keep the rain out of their faces, too. Paul stopped and rubbed his sore leg again and again. He hobbled beside Michael as they made their way through the blowing rain and howling wind.

It felt like they'd never reach Michael's house. But finally they turned onto his street. Michael looked up. His living-room curtains were parted, and his mother was peering out. As soon as she saw them, she opened the front door.

"Come inside. You're drenched to the bone." She hustled the boys into the house. She thrust two giant towels into their hands. "Leave your wet coats and boots in the furnace room."

The boys shook the water from their coats onto the mat inside the front hall and pulled off their wet boots.

"I wish your father didn't have to work late tonight," said Michael's mom. "The weather is getting worse by the minute."

"Maybe Mr. Trent will let him come home early," said Michael. Michael's dad was a carpenter and had a second job at a gas station three evenings a week.

Michael's mom sighed. "I doubt it. Mr. Trent likes to keep the station open as late as possible, especially in bad weather."

Paul held on to the railing as they headed down the narrow stairs to the basement. He stopped midway down, clenched the railing and bit his lip. Then he slowly continued down the rest of the stairs.

"Is your leg still sore?" asked Michael, as they placed their wet boots beside the furnace.

"Yeah," said Paul. "Flying garbage cans are dangerous."

The boys hung their wet coats on the indoor clothesline over the sink across from the furnace. Then they headed back upstairs to the kitchen.

"Here, this will warm you up," said Michael's mom. She handed each boy a steaming cup of cocoa with a giant marshmallow floating on top.

"Thanks, Mrs. Gordon!" said Paul, taking a sip. "I'd better call home right away. I promised to tell my parents that we arrived safely. You know my mom. She's a worrier, especially in bad weather."

Paul dialed his home number. "Hi, Mom. Yes. I'm fine. Really, I am. I'll see you tomorrow at noon."

"Come on. Let's go upstairs and start that Monopoly game before dinner," said Michael. "I have my lucky shirt ready."

Paul grinned. "I brought my lucky shirt, too. Tonight's my night to win. I can feel it in my bones."

"I can feel the win, too," said Michael.

"Supper at six," said Michael's mom. "It's beef stew and rice — perfect for a day like today." She walked over to the kitchen window and peered out. "I wish this rain would stop. Your dad is going to have a terrible time driving home later."

"The puddles were already as big as lakes when we walked home from school," said Michael. "Maybe this *is* Hurricane Hazel."

"I listened to the radio before you came home from school, and no one said anything about hurricanes," said Michael's mom. "It's just a lot of rain and wind. We'll be fine."

"Your mom is right," said Paul.

"I hope so," said Michael.

CHAPTER SIX

As soon as they reached Michael's room, Michael changed into his lucky shirt. His grandmother had given him the shirt for his birthday last year. It was red plaid with two deep pockets in front. He always wore it when he and Paul played Monopoly.

Paul yanked his lucky blue checked shirt from his overnight bag and put it on. His aunt had bought it for him for Christmas, and he wore it every time they played Monopoly.

The boys set up the game board on the grey rug between the two beds.

"Let the game begin!" Michael announced in a deep voice. He always did that before they began to play.

An hour later, they were still playing. Each

boy had bought three properties and had collected rent on some.

"Come down and help me set the table for dinner," Michael's mom called from the first floor.

"We'll be right there!" Michael stood up. "I'll break the tie later."

"You don't *know* that. I'm going to break the tie later!" said Paul, as they made their way to the kitchen.

Soon everyone was digging into heaping bowls of stew and rice around the kitchen table.

"How about some warm apple pie with vanilla ice cream for dessert?" said Michael's mom when they'd finished the main course.

"Yes, please," said the boys in unison.

Michael's mom gave them each a large slice of homemade pie and a big scoop of vanilla ice cream.

"This is delicious, Mrs. Gordon," said Paul, scooping up the last crumb of pie.

"It's the best," said Michael, as the boys helped clear the table.

"Listen!" said Michael's mom. "The rain's almost stopped and the wind's died down. Maybe this miserable storm is finally over."

"Let's go," said Michael. "Time to play!"

"Don't stay up too late. I'm going to watch TV and then curl up with a good book. Your father should be home before midnight."

"Goodnight, Mom," said Michael.

"Goodnight, Mrs. Gordon," said Paul.

"Goodnight, boys. I hope this storm is finally over. I hope we wake up to a beautiful clear day."

*　*　*

Two and a half hours later the rain came down hard again, the wind pounded against Michael's window and the game was still going. Michael had bought three more properties and Paul had bought four. It was Paul's turn to roll the dice.

He shook the dice in his right hand, then he

blew on them twice. "Come on, dice. Give me luck. I only need—" But before he could toss the dice, the lights in Michael's room went out. "Nuts! The light can't go out *now*."

"The wind must be hitting the electrical poles," said Michael.

"I wish it would stop ruining our game!" said Paul.

A minute later the lights were back on.

"Hooray!" said Paul.

But soon the lights flickered again.

Paul groaned.

"Don't worry, we can still play even if the lights go out. Look!" Michael crawled under his bed and fished out two flashlights.

"Great, but why do you have two?"

"In case one conks out. You know what Mr. Briggs said last week: 'Be prepared.'"

"Well, I'm prepared to win tonight!" Paul tossed the dice. "Three! I'm going to pass GO again. Two hundred dollars, Mr. Banker." He held out his palm.

Michael handed Paul $200. Then he tossed the dice. "Four! Thank you, dice!" Michael punched the air with his fist. "Now I'll pass GO too and collect two hundred dollars."

Michael counted out the money and paid himself as the lights flickered off and on again and again. Finally they didn't go back on at all. Michael flipped on a flashlight.

"I can't see well," said Paul, squinting. "It's hard to play by flashlight and I'm getting tired."

"Me too," Michael yawned. He flashed his light on the clock beside his bed. "It's eleven. No wonder we're tired, especially after we slogged through all that rain and wind."

"Let's finish the game in the morning. My mom's not coming to pick me up until noon."

"We can leave the Monopoly board on my desk and wake up early. We'll see who wins tomorrow. I'm going to wear my lucky shirt over my pyjamas to keep my luck going all night."

Paul yawned. "Yeah, me too. I can wait one more day to win!" As he scrambled up from the floor, he groaned.

"Is your leg still sore?" asked Michael, hopping into his bed close to the door.

Paul nodded. "Who'd believe I'd get clunked in the leg by a garbage can? And who'd believe it would hurt so much?"

"This is the craziest storm ever," said Michael.

CHAPTER SEVEN

"What was *that*?" Michael popped his eyes open. He bolted up in bed.

"Huh? What?" muttered Paul, turning over.

"Didn't you hear the bang?"

"Too sleepy. Go away," said Paul. He dragged the blanket over his ears.

"I'm going down. I'll be right back," said Michael.

"Okay," mumbled Paul.

Michael crawled out of bed and grabbed his flashlight. He flicked the light switch in the hallway. It wasn't working. The electricity was still out. He made his way down the stairs, aiming his flashlight ahead of him.

The wind screeched throughout the house. Rain pounded against the roof. Tree branches rapped against the windows. Garbage cans rattled outside the back door. Michael shivered.

Michael stopped midway down the steps and aimed his light toward the living room. It was hard to see anything clearly, despite his flashlight.

Another thud shook the house.

What was that?

Michael took another step down. The wind sounded like it was blasting right through the house. And there was a strange dripping noise. It sounded like it was inside their house, too.

Doesn't anyone else hear the banging and dripping?

Michael took another step and aimed his flashlight toward the living room.

"Oh no!" he gasped. The trunk of the large tree in the front yard had split in half and smashed the living-room window. Glass littered the room! Wet leaves and branches were strewn across the furniture. Pillows, broken lamps, shattered glass bowls and half of his mom's favourite vase floated down the living-room floor toward the kitchen. Water was gushing in through what was left of the broken window.

"Mom! Help!" he cried.

There was no answer.

"Help!" he screamed louder. "The house is flooding!"

"What happened?" His mother hurried out of her bedroom. She fastened her pink robe as she raced to the top of the stairs.

Michael pointed his flashlight toward the living room. "Look!"

"Oh my goodness!" His mom's eyes widened as she stared at the first floor. She sucked in her breath and clutched the stair railing. "Oh no. No! What are we going to do?" She dashed down the stairs toward Michael.

Paul stumbled out of Michael's bedroom and called down. "What's going on?" He rubbed his eyes.

"The house is flooding!" shouted Michael.

Paul headed downstairs. Halfway down he slipped on a step. He grabbed the railing and limped to the next step.

"We need help!" said Michael's mom. "I'll be right back. Hand me the flashlight. We need to call your dad. The neighbours. Someone."

Michael gave his mom the flashlight. She sloshed

across the soggy carpet to the kitchen. Her robe dragged in the water.

She was back in a minute.

"The phone is out!" she shouted. "The river has overflowed its banks and the street is flooded. Smashed cars are drifting in the water. We have to go up! We have to get out of here."

"Where can we go?" asked Michael.

"We have to go higher. Now. Oh, I wish your dad were here." His mom bit her lip. "I wish we knew he was safe."

"Dad's probably trying to get home."

His mom straightened up. "You're right, Michael. Come on!"

As they rushed upstairs, screams and cries echoed from outside.

"Help!"

"Our house is breaking apart."

"Save us."

"My dog!"

"Joe? Joe! Where are you?"

Michael shuddered. The whole neighbourhood was in trouble.

He glanced down. The bottom steps were immersed in water. The water in the house was rising higher and higher.

Another thud shook the house.

His mom turned. She flashed her light down and gasped.

A wave of water had crashed through their front door. Jagged wooden slabs floated toward the kitchen.

Their house shook again, but harder this time. The floor felt like it was shifting.

"Wh— What was that? Is the house moving?" asked Paul.

"I . . . I . . . hope not," said Michael.

"Let's go," said his mom.

They ran up to the second floor. Water covered half the stairs below them. It was rising faster and faster. Soon Michael's room, his parents' bedroom, the hall, the closets, the bathroom — everything on the second floor would be underwater, too. They had to get up higher. But what could they do? Where could they go? There was only one place.

And that's when the house tilted.

CHAPTER EIGHT

Michael's mom's face turned white. "The house *is* moving."

"Look! The water is almost at the top of the stairs! We have to get up higher," said Michael. "We have to . . ."

"I know. The attic to the roof. Hurry!"

"Wait! I'll be right back," said Michael. Before his mother could protest, he raced to his bedroom and grabbed his other flashlight. "Let's go!" he said.

His mom positioned the small ladder from the hall closet against the attic opening. She hurried up the four steps, lowered the opening to the attic and scrambled inside.

"Ouch," said Paul, as he bent his sore leg to climb inside, too.

Michael followed his friend. As he did he glanced down. Water was rising above the second floor landing and sloshing into the hall and bed-rooms. Michael pulled the opening to the attic shut behind him.

Michael's mom shivered. "It's freezing in here." She coughed. "And dusty. Watch out. Don't bang your head. The ceiling is low. Follow me."

The room was full of boxes of books and old clothing, crates of old record albums, a wooden toy chest, two rickety wooden chairs and a small metal table. There was little room to move.

The rain drummed overhead. They were so close to the roof, the wind whooshed right in their ears. The thick boards of the wooden floor creaked.

Suddenly the house tilted further, knocking them against boxes and furniture. The floor felt like it was going to collapse.

Michael looked at his mother. Her face was tight

and drawn. He knew she was thinking the same thing as he was. What if the house lifted off its foundation and drifted down the raging, cold river?

"There's no time. We have to get on the roof," said Michael's mom.

She scrambled over the cardboard boxes. She shimmied over the chest toward the attic window. She tried opening the window but it wouldn't budge. She rattled the frame, she pushed and prodded, but the window wouldn't open.

"It's stuck," she said. "I need something to break it."

Michael looked around. He lifted the lid of the wooden chest full of old toys. On top lay a small baseball bat he'd played with when he was little.

"Here!" he said, handing the bat to his mother.

"Good. Here goes." She pulled the bat back over her right shoulder. "Stand back." She swung the bat hard against the glass. The glass cracked but it didn't break.

She lifted the bat higher and slammed down harder. Nothing. She pursed her lips, grasped the bat tighter in her hands and came down hard on the glass.

It shattered. Glass flew everywhere. Michael's mom snapped off a large piece of the sharp broken glass still stuck to the window frame and placed it against the wall of the attic. She forced more glass from the frame.

"Ouch," she cried, rubbing her hand. A sharp piece of glass had cut her right hand.

Michael crawled over to a box of old clothes. He yanked out old jackets, scarves, tuques, socks and gloves. He handed some to his mother and Paul. His mom wrapped the scarf around her hand as showers of rain streamed through the broken attic window. A trickle of blood seeped through the scarf.

"We have to move quickly." Michael's mom aimed the flashlight out the window.

The floor tilted more. It creaked with every movement.

"Did you feel that? I don't know how long before the house is totally flooded. We have to climb out."

A sour taste rose up in Michael's throat. The

roof was steep. What would they hold on to out there? His knees felt weak. The bad taste rose higher. He tried swallowing it away but it kept coming back.

The house shook again. The floor tilted further. Michael glanced at Paul. Paul was biting his lip.

"I'll go first," said Michael's mom. "I'll see what's out there. Follow me quickly."

She tightened the thin scarf around her bleeding right hand. She put on a jacket, slid her feet into the socks and stuck the gloves into one of the deep pockets of her robe. She shoved one of the rickety chairs close to the window.

"Be careful, mom," said Michael. He directed his flashlight toward her. His mom pulled a tuque on her head and dropped the flashlight into the other pocket of her robe. She tightened her robe and climbed up on the chair. The chair wobbled.

His mom shivered. "Here goes. Keep your flashlight steady, Michael. Follow me out quickly, boys.

Don't wait." She took a deep breath and lowered herself out the window.

Michael peered out the broken window. The rain hammered the roof and hit him in the face. Where was his mother? He couldn't see anything. All he could hear was the rain pounding against the shingles and the wind howling.

"Mom? Mom! Where are you?"

His mom didn't answer.

"Mom!" he shouted again.

And then he heard her voice. It was faint. He could only make out a few words.

". . . antenna . . . vent . . . Go!"

Michael and Paul looked at each other. Michael's head throbbed so hard he couldn't think. His stomach hurt like someone had stepped on it. The sour taste rose up again. He glanced at Paul. He was trembling. They were both terrified but they had no choice. They had to get on the roof quickly.

"Go, Paul. I'll follow," he said.

"I . . . I . . ." stammered Paul.

"There isn't time," said Michael. "Now. Hurry."

Paul put on a jacket, tuque and gloves. His eyes were wide with fear.

Michael aimed the flashlight out. The sky was steely grey. Giant clouds looked like they'd explode.

Michael glanced up. The rain slowed for a minute and he could see his mother! She crouched on the sloping roof of their house, clinging to the TV antenna with both hands. Rain poured down her hair, her face, her robe.

"Come on, Paul," she cried. "The roof slopes but you can lean against it. There's a plumbing vent sticking out. Grab it. You can make it." She shone her flashlight toward him.

Paul's hand shook as he climbed up on the chair. He looked out. He groaned as he bent his knees on the window ledge. The chair fell back as Paul lowered himself out of the window.

CHAPTER NINE

Paul inched his way across the wet roof. He grabbed the thick metal pipe jutting out. He clung to it and leaned against the roof.

"I made it," he called out. "Go, Michael."

Michael's mom shone her flashlight toward the attic window.

Michael put on a jacket and stuck his flashlight into a side pocket. He buttoned the pocket and pulled on a tuque. He picked up the chair and positioned it back near the window. His legs shook as he climbed up. The chair wobbled. He leaned forward and looked out the window. As he did, the chair snapped and Michael fell back. He tumbled into a box, banging his right shoulder on a sharp edge. His shoulder throbbed.

It felt like it was on fire. He rubbed it then he pulled himself up.

The floor creaked and heaved.

Michael's hands trembled as he pulled over the other rickety chair. He held on to it with one hand and yanked himself up with the other. The chair swayed like a seesaw.

"Michael, where are you? What happened?" His mother's frantic voice rose above the pelting rain.

"Michael! Hurry!" called Paul. "I think the water's rising higher in the house."

Michael's heart was beating so hard he couldn't think. He peered out the window. Paul leaned against the wet shingles and clung to the pipe. His mother crouched on the roof above Paul and held on tightly to the TV antenna. Their faces dripped with the pounding rain. The wind snapped against their clothing.

Someone screamed from below.

"Help me! Please!"

More screams pierced the darkness. Screams echoed over the rain and wind.

"Go, Michael!" called his mother. "Now!"

Michael could barely breathe. The sour taste rose in his mouth.

Don't look down. Don't think. Go.

He lowered himself out the window feet first.

His rear end dragged along the slippery shingles. As he made his way slowly toward his mother and Paul, his right foot slid on a loose shingle.

He was sliding!

He reached for something — anything — to stop him from falling off the roof, but there was nothing to hold on to. Nothing.

He fell into the darkness and splashed into the icy water.

The water filled his mouth. It filled his nose. He couldn't breathe.

He pushed himself up. Up.

He gasped for air. He spit out mouthfuls of foul-tasting water.

Swim. Swim. You can.

But it was so hard to move. The swirling, fast-moving water spun him around and around.

The current was powerful. It was pulling him down. He was going under again.

No. No. Stay up.

He flapped his arms. He pumped his legs. He forced his head up.

He could hear screams from the darkness. They echoed around him.

Breathe. Breathe. You can swim. You know how.

Something large was floating toward him. It was coming close. Very close. It spun. It hit him in the side.

A garage door!

Michael grabbed the edge of the door. He tried to hoist himself up on it but it was too high, too slippery. He tried again. Again his hands slipped off.

Oh no!

The door was spinning away down the river.

Michael swam toward the door. *Yes!* He could touch it. He grabbed the side of the door again and, with all his might, pulled himself onto it.

He lay on the rough wood door. He wrapped his right hand tightly around one side of it and slowly sat up. Some of the wood had fallen off and the door was splintery, uneven.

Michael took deep breaths. He had to stay on the door, but it bumped up and down and around in the churning water. It never stopped moving. It was like a non-stop roller coaster at the fair, and his stomach felt like it was rolling with it. The sour taste rose up in his throat.

The door flew past floating houses wrenched off their foundations. It banged into debris that Michael was sure came from the houses destroyed by the storm.

Michael peered into the dark night. It was hard to see anything. Then he remembered his flashlight. It was in his jacket pocket, but would it still work?

His hands trembled as he tried to undo the button. The cloth was so wet it was hard to push the button through the hole, and his fingers were numb from the cold. But finally he did.

He reached deep into the pocket and pulled out the flashlight. It was wet. His hand shook as he flipped the switch on.

The flashlight still worked! The light wasn't strong, but he could see around him. Michael gasped as he identified some of the debris — part of a bed frame, a tabletop, roof shingles, even a bathtub!

Where was he? Where were his mother and Paul? Nothing looked familiar. The door suddenly spun wildly like a top. Michael quickly shoved the flashlight back into his pocket. He couldn't lose it.

The door kept spinning and spinning. Michael's head throbbed. He felt dizzy and cold. His hands and feet were icy and numb. He couldn't think.

Hold on. Hold on.

The door swirled round in the current. The bitter, sour taste rose higher in Michael's throat. He held on tightly to the side of the door, leaned over the edge and threw up into the water. Then he raised his head and sat up.

He sucked in mouthfuls of air as the spinning slowed down. He took more long breaths. He felt less queasy, but the chill and the damp made him shiver. He couldn't stop shivering.

And then with a hard bang the door hit the side of a house. The door tilted. Michael's hand flew off the side. He slid across the door.

He was headed straight for the water.

CHAPTER TEN

Michael dug in his heels and grabbed the sides of the door. He pushed himself up toward the end snagged on the house. The door banged into the house again, but this time more lightly. The door bobbed up and down but it didn't tip into the churning water.

How can there be a house in the middle of the river? thought Michael.

Before he could figure it out, the strength of the current tore the door free of the house and sent it down the river. Soon Michael couldn't see the house anymore. The rain pelted his face and his body. The wind screeched in his ears. Bangs, clangs and screams reverberated all around him.

A dog barked. It barked again and again. Each

bark grew louder. Michael looked up toward the barking. A dog stood on a roof that had been ripped off a house. The roof was spinning down the river toward Michael.

The dog looked familiar. Its long fur hung down like a mop. It looked like Rupert, a dog that lived down the street. It *was* Rupert.

Rupert always greeted Michael with licks when he passed the Langers' house. Rupert loved being patted on the head. He loved treats. Michael wished he could reach out and touch Rupert's head. He wished he could pat him on the back. He wished he could stroke his wet fur and tell him he wasn't alone.

"Hey, Rupert!" Michael called out, as the roof passed him.

Rupert barked again. Did he recognize Michael? He barked again and again. He walked back and forth on the roof, almost falling into the water. But each time the roof tipped, Rupert regained his balance.

Was that the Langers' roof? Was the rest of their house in the river, too? Where were the Langers?

Where was Michael's mother? And Michael's father? And Paul?

A wave of sadness rushed over Michael. He

wished he were back on the roof with his mother and Paul. Surely someone would come and rescue them from there. But where was this door taking him? How could he stay on it? When would it ever stop moving?

He bit his lip. Tears ran down his wet face. He couldn't stop thinking of his family and Paul. His mother and Paul had seen him fall off the roof. Did they see him climb on the door, or did they think he'd drowned?

Rupert's barks were growing fainter now. Soon Michael couldn't see Rupert anymore. He could barely hear his barks.

He felt so alone, so tired.

Michael continued down the river, past a man on the roof of a car that was almost completely submerged in the river. The man clutched the inside of the window in order to stay on the roof. He shouted and pleaded for help. Michael called out to him. The man called back, but the wind and rain kept his words from Michael, and Michael kept going down the river.

Suddenly the door slowed down near a small clump of trees. Most of the trees were bashed and battered except for one. It was tall and had four thick trunks attached near the base. Many of the top branches were damaged or gone, but its four trunks were intact. The giant tree stood out of the water like a small island.

The door hit one of the trunks, causing it to slow down and bob up and down. Michael heard a faint sound. Was it a cat meowing, or was it just the wind?

And then a large pile of debris rushed by, making the door hit the tree with a thud.

The door creaked. Michael looked down. The door was splitting in half. It was about to break into pieces!

CHAPTER ELEVEN

Michael leaned out as far as he could and grabbed one of the tree trunks. He pulled himself off the door just as it split in two. One piece of it spun away down the river. The other bounced against the tree again and again. Soon the door was little more than jagged pieces of floating wood.

Michael clung to the trunk. The rain was slowing down. The wind was still blowing but not as fiercely. Was the storm almost over? Would someone come looking for him? If he could get up higher in the tree he'd stand a better chance of being seen.

"Meow."

There was that meowing sound again. He looked up. Above him one of the tree trunks had divided in two, creating a space that looked like a small seat. The meowing was coming from close to there.

Michael clambered up the tree. The bark was as wet and slippery as the roof of his house had been, but he kept going. He climbed higher and higher until he reached the seat.

Michael squeezed himself into the narrow space. It was tight. He had to scrunch his legs in together, but he fit.

"Meow."

It was a cat, but where was it? It was too dark to see. Michael touched the pocket on his jacket. The flashlight was still there! He fumbled with the button until he undid it then carefully pulled the flashlight out and shone it above him.

There was the cat! It was huddled on a thick branch right above the seat in the tree. It was medium sized and ginger coloured. Michael had seen a cat like that around the neighbourhood. He'd only noticed it a few times and he didn't know who owned it, but once it had come right up and rubbed against

Michael's leg. Michael had stroked it as it purred. Then the cat had scurried away down the block.

Could this be the same cat?

"Hi there!" he called up.

"Meow. Meow."

Michael leaned against the trunk. He was exhausted. His shoulders, his legs and his arms ached from climbing the tree. He snapped the flashlight off, stuck it back into his pocket and leaned back against the wet tree.

I'll just close my eyes for a minute.

As he did something brushed against his face.

He opened his eyes. It was the cat. It had scampered down and leaped into Michael's lap.

Michael patted it. It had a faded leather collar but no tag.

"What's your name?" he asked.

"Meow."

Michael smiled. "Meow's a good name. Nice to meet you, Meow."

As if the cat understood, it rubbed against Michael's arm.

"So what do we do now, Meow?" said Michael.

The cat purred and rubbed against Michael again. Then it curled itself into Michael's lap.

Michael patted the cat's head. It felt good to have some company. But he was still so tired. His eyes began to close again.

"Meow. Meow. Meow."

Michael opened his eyes. The cat licked his face. How long had he been asleep and what was that whirring sound?

Michael looked around. "What is that? It sounds like . . . a helicopter!"

A helicopter was circling above.

"Help! I'm here. In the tree," Michael yelled. "Please. Help!"

The whirring grew louder. The helicopter flew lower.

Michael yelled over and over till he was hoarse.

Did the pilot see him?

The whirring sounded so close now. It had to be right above him. He had to find a way to let the pilot know he was there. Michael fumbled with the button on his jacket. He pulled out the flashlight with one hand and held on to the tree with the other, then leaned away from the trunk. As he aimed the flashlight up toward the whirring sound, a strong blast of wind blew through. It tossed Michael back against the trunk and the flashlight flew out of his hand! It plunged down toward the churning water.

It was gone.

Meow huddled close to Michael and licked his face.

The helicopter whir grew fainter and fainter. It was flying away!

Soon Michael couldn't hear the helicopter at all. The only sounds were his pounding heart and the endless howling wind.

CHAPTER TWELVE

Meow purred and rubbed against Michael's arm and leg. It was as if the ginger cat knew how alone and scared Michael felt.

Michael patted Meow. He was glad the cat was beside him, but how long could he stay up in the tree?

He was too tired, too thirsty, too wet to think. The water stirred below. A small patch of light gleamed through the menacing grey clouds. It had to be close to dawn, but there was nowhere to go.

"Meow."

The cat brushed against his face again and again. *Brrr.*

A new sound, this time coming from below.

Michael looked down. It sounded like a motor. Could there be a boat down there? He peered through the dim light, but it was too hard to see.

He listened again.

The sound was louder, clearer now. It *was* a motor. There had to be a boat down there.

Michael shouted for help, but his voice was low and hoarse. Could he be heard over the motor? Could he be heard over the wind? Would the boat stop near the tree? How would they see him if they couldn't hear him yell for help?

The motor grew louder and louder. Then the motor stopped.

Michael tried to shout again. "Please. I'm up a tree. Please come and help me!"

"Is someone there?" a voice from below called up.

"My name is Michael. I'm in the big tree!"

"Hey, Ted. I think there's someone in that tree. Can you see anything up there?"

"Let's try and get closer," said Ted. "Then hand me that light and I'll aim it up the tree. I'm sure I heard someone."

"I don't know how long I can keep the boat steady in this current. Here's the light."

A beam of light shone on the bottom of the tree. The light moved higher, above the spot where Michael crouched.

Michael tried to scream again and again, but his voice was so hoarse now he knew the men couldn't hear him.

Suddenly Meow leaped out of Michael's lap and scurried up the tree to the spot where the light was shining.

"Hey, Ted! There's a cat in the tree. Wow. Look at it go!"

Meow scampered down from the upper branch back to where Michael was crouched.

The men lowered their light to follow the cat's movements.

"Look! Up there! There's a kid in the tree!" The men shone the light on Michael's perch.

"Hey, kid!" the man called out. "We see you. We're going to help you!"

Michael wanted to yell back, but all he could get out was a croak. All he could do was wait for the men to help him.

Michael waited. He couldn't hear anything but the wind.

Why weren't the men saying anything? Should he climb down from his perch, or were they coming up to get him?

Michael waited longer. Then he heard the motor again. Was the boat coming closer or going away? He couldn't tell from the sound.

Maybe he should climb down. Maybe that would make it easier to reach him. At least if he was closer to the bottom, they could tell him what to do next.

"Come on, Meow. We're getting out of here."

Michael picked the cat up. He slipped the squirming cat into his jacket. Then he grabbed the trunk of the tree and began to make his way slowly down. The ginger cat wiggled and wiggled till it squirmed out of Michael's jacket. Meow scurried down the tree.

"Meow. Where are you going?"

CHAPTER THIRTEEN

Meow scooted down to the bottom of the tree. The cat perched on a thick lower branch that hung over the water.

Michael lowered himself to the bottom of the tree. He settled on the branch beside Meow, with one arm wrapped around the trunk.

He heard the motor again. The boat was close now! He could see two men in the boat!

"Hey, kid. I'm Rick," called the burly, broad-shouldered man steering the boat. "This is Ted." A tall, skinny man waved to Michael.

"I'm Michael Gordon."

"Can you hold on a bit longer, Michael? We're coming."

"I'll try."

The rain had slowed down to a steady drizzle now, and the wind wasn't as loud as before, but Michael was so wet and tired it took all the energy he had left to cling to the slippery trunk.

The men steered the boat toward him, but the current pushed them back. They tried over and over to reach Michael. Finally they were able to steer close to the tree.

"Get in!" said Ted.

Michael picked up Meow with one arm and held on to the trunk with the other. "You'll be safe now," he told the squirming cat.

He reached out as far as he could and dropped Meow into Rick's arms.

Meow mewled and wiggled as Rick placed the cat in the boat.

"Now you, Michael," Rick called out. "Lean over. I'll grab you and hoist you into the boat."

Michael leaned forward, but just as he reached for Rick's hand, a pile of debris floated down the water and banged into the boat. The boat swerved and spun into the current.

"Wait. Don't worry. We're coming back," called Ted. The boat spun away from the tree.

The men aimed the boat toward the tree again, but the current forced it in the opposite direction. It drifted farther and farther away from Michael!

Michael's heart sank as he clung to the tree trunk. He couldn't stay on that branch much longer. He grabbed the trunk to take some of his weight off the branch. He didn't want to fall into the fast-moving, cold water.

He had to go higher up the tree again. But his arms and legs felt so weak.

He began to shiver. He couldn't stop shivering. When would they come back? They had to come soon.

Michael started climbing back up to his perch on the tree, but his hands and legs ached so much, he kept losing his hold of the damp bark. He tried again and again. His whole body hurt. His head throbbed. He felt dizzy but he kept climbing.

He was halfway up the trunk when someone called his name.

Rick and Ted were back! This time they were steering a larger boat.

"Come down, Michael. This boat has a stronger motor."

"I'm coming," said Michael.

Michael lowered himself down again. The boat neared the tree. The current kept pushing it away, but Rick and Ted wouldn't give up. They steered the larger boat as close to the tree as they could.

"Hurry!" said Rick. "Slide out to the end of the branch and jump in. You can do it!"

Michael looked down. The water swirled below him. His heart pounded as he inched across the slippery branch. Then he was right over the boat. With a quick movement, he leaped in.

His shirt caught on something sharp and tore as he stumbled into the boat. He sank into the small wooden seat in the back.

"Thank you," he said.

The men wrapped Michael in a warm blanket.

They handed him a Thermos of water. He took a long swig. The water tasted good. "Where's the cat?" he asked.

"Our friend took it to an animal shelter," said Rick.

"It's a great cat. Someone is probably looking for it."

Rick patted Michael on the back. "You took good care of it."

Michael leaned back against the wooden seat in the boat. He was glad the cat was safe. He was glad he was safe. But what about his family? What happened to them? What had happened to Paul?

"Can you please help me find my family? I don't know where they are or what's happened to them."

"We will. We promise," said Ted.

CHAPTER FOURTEEN

Michael closed his eyes. All he wanted to do was sleep.

The next thing he knew the boat had stopped. Rick was tying it to a dock.

"Here we are. Come on. We'll get someone from the Red Cross to find you some dry clothing and some breakfast and help you locate your family. A doctor should check you out, too. You look pale. You shivered all the way back."

❋   ❋   ❋

The next few hours were a blur. Michael was taken to a shelter set up to help victims of the storm. A lady from the Red Cross hurried over to help

Michael. She brought him a pair of jeans and a shirt that were way too big, but Michael didn't mind. The clothes were dry. She gave Michael a cheese sandwich and a container of milk. He asked her to help him find out what had happened to his family and Paul. She said she'd try but she explained that things were still confused. Lists of survivors were still being organized.

At 11 that morning a doctor examined Michael in a makeshift exam room. He took his temperature and checked his eyes, his nose and his pulse. He told Michael he was lucky. Given all that he'd been through he was in good shape. He just needed a few days of rest.

Michael thanked the doctor. He stood up.

"I don't know where to go now," he said. "I don't know where my family is or what's happened to them."

"Let's see what we can find out," said the doctor, walking Michael to the door of the room.

Before they could step out, a nurse rushed in. She whispered in the doctor's ear. "I see," said the doctor, smiling. "Michael, come with me."

The doctor led Michael to another room. "I think you'll have your answers now."

The door opened.

"Michael!" said his mom, rushing toward him. She wrapped him in her arms.

"Oh, son!" said his dad, hugging him tight.

Michael bit his lips. He didn't want to cry, but he was so happy to see his parents that he couldn't stop the tears.

"I was so worried about you both," he said. His voice cracked. "What happened on the roof, Mom? And, Dad, where were you?"

Their stories tumbled out between more hugs and tears. Michael's father had been stuck near the gas station. By the time he was finished with work and the gas station closed, the roads were flooded. It was impossible to drive home. He found some people with a boat, and they helped him get part of the way home. His dad had spent the rest of the night trying to find his family.

His mom and Paul had been rescued by boat soon after Michael fell into the water. They were taken to a church with many other victims of the storm. That's where Michael's dad had found them. A volunteer had called Paul's parents and they arrived shortly after to take Paul home.

Michael's parents had asked everyone at the shelter and all the Red Cross workers if they'd seen Michael or heard anything about what had happened to him. Until a few minutes ago, they had no news. All they could do was keep asking.

As they waited for news about Michael they heard that their house, along with many houses in their neighbourhood, had been destroyed. The family would never be able to live in their house again. They'd go back to the site when it was safe and see what they could salvage, but there probably wasn't much left.

"We've lost so much. But I can't tell you how relieved I was to see your mom and Paul and how worried I was when we didn't know where you were, Michael," said his dad.

"Where are we going to live now?" asked Michael.

"We'll stay with Paul's family. They said we could stay until we find a new place," his dad explained. "Luckily, their street didn't have much damage. Just some water in a few basements."

"They were grateful that we helped Paul get through this. He was shook up, but he's better now," said Michael's mom. "I saw you grab on to that garage door, Michael, but then I couldn't see you or the door anymore. I didn't know what happened. It was horrible." She began to cry.

"Don't cry, Mom. Please," said Michael. "I'm fine now."

"I hate thinking about what you must have gone through, but I'm so grateful that you were rescued. So many people came to help today."

CHAPTER FIFTEEN

By the following Wednesday Michael was back at school. So were most of the other kids. A few, including Michael, Ian and Jim, had lost their homes. Jim was back in class but Ian wasn't. Ian's grandmother had died in the storm. She'd been visiting them and had fallen down the stairs when their house collapsed. Ian and his family were staying with his grandfather in the country.

Emma, who sat behind Michael in class, had lost her dog. When he heard that, Michael thought of the Langers' dog, Rupert. Rupert had survived his wild ride on the roof and was back with the Langers. Their house had been severely damaged, and they were hunting for a new place to live. Michael's neighbourhood and all the people who'd lived there would never be the same.

Two kids in his class and their families had moved in with relatives outside Toronto and weren't coming back to school for a while.

But the class had decided that the speech contest would go on as planned.

"You picked the perfect topic — hurricanes," Mr. Briggs said to Michael before morning recess. "Who would have believed that Toronto would be hit by one?"

The bell rang. Michael and Paul hurried outside.

"Let's play Monopoly tonight," said Paul. "We have to finally break that tie. I'm going to win, even though my lucky blue shirt is too messed up from the storm to wear again. I feel the win in my bones."

"Don't count on it," said Michael, laughing. "I feel a win in *my* bones too, even without my lucky shirt."

"Well, we'll see whose bones are right," said Paul.

The friends laughed and hurried to their favourite spot in the yard to play catch. They'd been playing for ten minutes when Paul said, "Hey, Michael! Look who's coming over."

Michael spun around. It was Jim. What did Jim want? It was his first day back to school, too. He hadn't said a word to Michael — or to anyone. Mr. Briggs had asked him if he was feeling well and he said yes, but something was different.

Maybe it was because Ian wasn't around. Maybe it was because Jim was sad about losing his house and everything in it. Michael didn't know how Jim had been rescued. All Michael knew was that everyone in Jim's family had made it out alive.

"I'm sorry about your house," said Michael.

"Yeah. Sorry about yours, too. I heard you had a rough time during the storm. I heard you were stranded up a tree and that you were really . . . brave."

"It was tough out there. I was on the roof first and then I got stuck up a tree."

"With a cat, right?"

Michael and Paul looked at each other. How did Jim know?

"Who told you?" asked Michael.

"This lady named Francine who runs the animal shelter told us about it. The cat you rescued was our cat, Ginger."

Michael's eyes widened. Rick had called Paul's house two days after Michael was rescued to find out how he was doing. He'd told Michael that the cat's owner had been found. And now he knew who that was — Jim!

"She's a great cat," said Michael. "She kept me company in the tree and helped get us rescued."

Jim smiled. "She's smart. My little brother, Herbie, wouldn't stop crying when we thought we lost her. We got out of our house early in the storm but Ginger disappeared. We asked everybody if they'd seen her but no one had. We checked at the animal shelter and she wasn't there. We tried again a few hours later and there she was! Francine at the shelter told us how you took care of Ginger. She said you made sure she was rescued, even before you were helped out of the tree. So I just wanted to say . . . thanks. Once we're settled in a new place, you could come visit her, if you want."

"Thanks. I'd like that."

"Okay." Jim turned and walked back toward the school building.

The bell rang.

"Wow!" said Michael. "Do you believe what just happened? Ginger is Jim's cat, and he said thanks — to me."

"You should talk about that in your speech on hurricanes on Friday. Everyone loves a story with a happy ending."

"I don't know what I'll say in my speech," said Michael. "I only know one thing: it's different when you live through a disaster than when you read about it."

CHAPTER SIXTEEN

As soon as Michael woke up on the day of the speech contest his stomach hurt. Today was the day he'd speak in front of the class. He wished he had his lucky red shirt to help him get through it, but it was too ripped to wear again.

He was prepared for the speech. He'd read books and articles on hurricanes. He'd read all the latest newspaper reports on Hurricane Hazel. He'd practised his speech ten times in front of the mirror in Paul's basement, but he was still nervous about speaking.

Paul had told him he'd do a good job. His parents said he'd be great. He knew the information, so why was his stomach still doing flip-flops like an acrobat in the circus?

He was going to be the first speaker. That was good and bad. It was good that he'd get his speech over with before Jim went up to talk about motorcycles and Paul spoke about sharks. They were both confident speakers, and it would be harder listening to them and waiting for his turn.

But it was bad because there was no time left. In only a few hours Michael would speak.

He tried not to think about it as he and Paul hurried to school, but the worry kept sneaking in.

Before Michael knew it, Mr. Briggs was calling on him to come up to the front of the room.

Michael's heart raced.

You know your speech, he told himself, as he walked up. His knees shook all the way up to the front of the room.

He cleared his throat. He coughed twice.

Then he began:

No one expected a hurricane to hit Toronto. Everyone thought that hurricanes only slam into places like the Caribbean, Florida, the southern American states or Mexico. No one believed that a hurricane could reach this far north.

On October 15 nothing happened the way we expected. Hurricane Hazel blew into Toronto. I'll never forget what happened to my house, my family, my friends and my neighbourhood when that hurricane surprised us. I'll never forget that eighty-one people died and many people were injured. I'll never forget that almost 2000 people lost their homes. I was one of them, and so were some of you.

But I'll also never forget that people came out in the pouring, pounding rain, the fierce howling wind and the bitter, damp cold to rescue us. It was danger-ous to go anywhere that night. The electricity was off in many parts of the city. The suspension bridge over the Humber that many of us crossed on the way to school broke, and parts of the bridge battered many of the flooded houses. The current in the raging Humber was so strong that many boats couldn't reach people in need of help.

My mom and Paul helped me climb onto our roof, but I fell into the water. It was scary and cold, but I was lucky. A door spun past me, and I pulled myself onto it. A few hours later the door broke, but I climbed up a tree. A sweet cat named Ginger, who was stuck up in the tree with me, helped me stay calm. She even helped us be seen by a rescue boat by meowing and racing up and down the tree. I didn't know it then, but I do now. That cat belongs to Jim in our class.

Since the day the hurricane struck, I've heard about lots of amazing people like Rick and Ted who rescued me. Some people dashed out to help their neighbours and were stranded themselves and had to be rescued, too. It was so hard to reach people that the military was called out to help. Firemen and policemen risked their lives. Five firemen from the Kingsway-Lambton Fire Station were killed trying to rescue people stranded in cars.

A man in Woodbridge saved twenty-seven cats and fourteen dogs. A policeman, Jim Crawford, and his brother Pat, who weren't working that night, got a boat and rescued fifty people from porches and windows. A helicopter picked up Mr. and Mrs. Joseph Ward in our Weston neighbourhood.

Doctors and nurses worked extra hours to take care of the injured.

Toronto didn't expect a hurricane. We weren't prepared for one, but in the end I'm proud of our city, and I'm happy that everyone in our class made it through that terrible day.

Michael sat down. The class applauded loudly and long. Paul and Jim flashed him the V-for-victory sign.

Michael beamed.

It was amazing!

Once he started talking his knees had stopped shaking, his heart had stopped pounding and, best of all, the words had poured out.

Author's Note

When Hurricane Hazel hit Toronto on October 15, 1954, it took the city by surprise. No one expected a hurricane to travel this far north, but a combination of unusual conditions made Hazel take a deadly detour. The storm that originated over the Atlantic Ocean around October 5 pummelled Haiti, the Carolinas and the suburbs of Washington, DC. It sped north, taking an unexpected 1100 km path over land, and merged with a cold front over Pennsylvania. Then it veered northwest and slammed into Toronto.

By this time Hazel had been downgraded from a category 4 hurricane to an extra-tropical storm. Despite its lower ranking, Hazel was still powerful and destructive. To make matters worse, Toronto had little experience with hurricanes. The city was unprepared for the endless rain and pounding winds. The clay soil, already soaked from days of non-stop rain, was saturated by more rain. Rivers and streams already higher than normal overflowed their banks.

All these conditions resulted in massive flooding. Houses were yanked off their foundations, cars were stranded in deep water, unstable bridges broke apart and many people were caught in situations beyond their control.

Hurricane! is set in the Weston area of Toronto, a neighbourhood near the Humber River. Weston was one of the hardest-hit areas in the city. On Raymore Drive, a street near the Humber, over thirty people died, sixty families were left homeless and fourteen houses were destroyed.

Here's how David Phillips, an eyewitness to the events on Raymore Drive, described what happened that night: "I could see the houses tumbling into the river. I ran down to the river to try and help, but there was nothing we could do. We tried to get a boat, but the water was too rough . . . And the water just kept coming. We were forced to stand there and watch people die."

Raymore Drive, once a quiet residential street, was so devastated during Hurricane Hazel that it was never rebuilt. It is now parkland.

Houses floating down the Humber River during the aftermath of Hurricane Hazel

Facts About Hurricane Hazel

- Hurricane Hazel was officially "born" near the island of Grenada, close to South America, around October 5, 1954.
- Hazel was the eighth tropical storm that year.
- Between 400 and 1000 people died in Haiti during Hurricane Hazel, and almost half the coffee and cacao crops were destroyed.
- About 100 people died in the United States as a result of Hurricane Hazel. It destroyed the entire town of Garden City, South Carolina.

- In Ontario eighty-one people died, about 1900 people were left homeless and there were millions of dollars in damages. Many consider Hazel the worst natural disaster in Canadian history.

- Hurricanes are rated on a score of 1 to 5 on the Saffir-Simpson Hurricane Wind Scale. The most powerful and destructive hurricanes receive a 5 rating. Hurricane Katrina, which slammed into the southern US states in 2005, is an example of a Category 3 hurricane. The hurricane with the least potential for damage receives a 1 rating.

- At one point, Hazel was a category 4 hurricane, but as it moved north it was given a lower score. Although Hazel was downgraded to below hurricane status, it still triggered extensive flooding in Ontario.

- The "eye of a hurricane" is an eerie time of calm in the middle of a hurricane. It doesn't mean that the hurricane is over. Instead — watch out — there's probably more destructive wind and rain to come.

- The area around the Humber River in the Weston area of Toronto was vulnerable to flooding because it was flat and there were few trees to help absorb the heavy rainfall.

- Forty highways and main roads were under water in the Toronto area after Hazel. The hurricane knocked passenger trains off their tracks and destroyed or severely damaged forty bridges.

- Many meteorologists, the scientists who study weather, consider a fully developed hurricane to be the most destructive of all storms. Unlike tornadoes, which affect a narrow band of territory, hurricanes can cause massive damage over a wide area.

- The word *hurricane* came into use after three Spanish ships sailing near the Island of Santo Domingo in 1495 were caught in a violent storm and sank to the bottom of the sea. The survivors of that storm adopted a local word, *huracán,* to describe what happened, and the word spread.
- Tropical storms are given names, and if they turn into a hurricane they keep their tropical storm name.
- Calling a hurricane by name makes it easier to talk about the storm. Before 1953, hurricanes were given the names of the year in which they occurred plus a letter. For example: 1933A, 1933B. For many years after 1953, hurricanes were given female names like Hazel. In 1979 hurricanes were given alternating female and male names. Hurricane names begin with all letters of the alphabet except for Q, U, X, Y and Z since

there are few names beginning with those letters.

- As a result of the destruction during Hazel, Toronto developed a plan for flood control and water conservation.

ALSO AVAILABLE

ISBN 978-1-4431-4638-8

In a matter of seconds, Alex's world is turned up-side down. What started out as the perfect day to build an epic snow fort turns into his worst night-mare. Injured and disoriented, can Alex find his classmates trapped in the deadly snow?

ALSO AVAILABLE

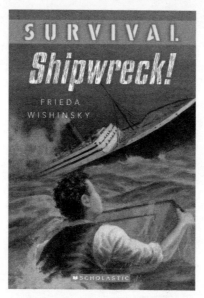

ISBN 978-1-4431-4641-8

Albert and Grace feel a jolt. The *Empress of Ireland* begins to tilt. People scream. Stewards order passengers to head for the lifeboats. Water rushes into the ship as passengers race to the top deck. The ship tilts toward the water. Lifeboats crash down. Grace and Albert have no choice. They leap into the St. Lawrence River.